CARTOON NETWORK™

SCOOBY-DOO
AND THE
LOCH NESS MONSTER

Adapted by Jesse Leon McCann
from the script by Douglas Wood

WORLDWIDE PUBLISHING ™

SCHOLASTIC INC.
New York   Toronto   London   Auckland   Sydney
Mexico City   New Delhi   Hong Kong   Buenos Aires

MW01010499

Dedicated to my wonderful new bride, Nancy McCann.
Thanks for brightening my life.

ISBN 0-439-60697-7

Cover designed by Louise Bova, interior designed by Maria Stasavage.
Special thanks to Duendes del Sur for interior illustrations.
Printed in the U.S.A.
First printing, June 2004

12 11 10 9 8 7 6 5 4   5 6 7 8 9/0

Scooby-Doo and the Mystery, Inc. gang were in Scotland to visit Daphne's cousin Shannon. Shannon lived in a huge castle on the shores of a giant lake called Loch Ness.

"I'm so excited!" Daphne said. "I can't wait to help cousin Shannon host the Loch Ness Highland Games!"

"Wow!" exclaimed Shaggy. "Look at all those tents! I wonder if there's a circus in town." "That's the sports field for the Highland Games, a competition featuring traditional Scottish sporting events," Velma explained.

"Shannon!" Daphne ran to give her cousin a big hug. "I can't believe I'm really here!"

"Daphne!" Shannon said eagerly, turning away from some men putting a patch over a big hole in Shannon's boat.

Shannon's boat had been damaged by something in the lake. Something big! As she and the gang examined the hole, a man named Del rushed up. Del was certain the legendary Loch Ness Monster really existed.

"It's because of the Highland Games!" Del cried. "All the activity has disturbed the creature!"

"Zoinks!" Shaggy cried.

The gang followed Shannon into Blake Castle. "No one here has ever had any trouble with the monster," Shannon explained. "That is, until now!"

A few nights earlier, Shannon had heard a strange noise outside. Suddenly, the windows had crashed open and the Loch Ness Monster burst in! ROAR!

Shaggy and Scooby were so frightened by Shannon's story, they leaped into a suit of armor!

Scooby and his pals weren't the only guests at Blake Castle. Sir Ian Locksley and Professor Fiona Pembroke were visiting, too. They were both experts on the Loch Ness Monster. But Sir Ian thought the monster legend was phony and Professor Pembroke was sure the sea creature was real. They argued about it all the time.

After bedtime, Scooby and Shaggy went in search of a midnight snack. The castle was ten times spookier at night!

"Like, how far is it to the nearest vending machine?" Shaggy gulped.

They didn't find any snacks, but they did find trouble. Without meaning to, they got themselves locked outside the castle. And they weren't alone!

ROAR! It was the Loch Ness Monster!

Shaggy and Scooby ran as fast as they could. They raced through the Highland Games area. The beast followed, crushing tents as it went. Scooby and Shaggy were as scared as they could be!

"Roooh!" Scooby cried.

Later, when the others found **Shaggy** and **Scooby** hiding under a collapsed tent, the monster was long gone — and the games area was in shambles.

"Jinkies!" Velma exclaimed when she saw the creature's huge footprints.

"Well, gang," Fred said. "It looks like we've got another mystery on our hands."

In town, Shannon asked the innkeeper and his sons Angus and Colin for help. They agreed to help her repair all the damage the monster had caused.

Angus and Colin were big practical jokers. As they left, they gave the ropes of a Loch Ness Monster balloon to Shaggy and Scooby. Moments later, Shaggy and Scooby found themselves pulled high into the sky by the big balloon!

The gang's next step was to search the lake. Sir Ian agreed to let them use his ship, which had a mini-submarine onboard. The kids decided to take the sub and look for the monster underwater.

"Hang on, folks!" Fred commanded from the pilot's seat. "It's time for splashdown!"

Soon they were diving deep below the loch's surface. The lake was very murky, which made it hard to navigate. A monster could hide anywhere.

Scooby suddenly glimpsed a scary-looking eel outside. "Ronster! Ronster!" he cried.

He grabbed onto Fred, causing Fred to steer the sub wildly. By sheer luck, Fred piloted them right into an underwater cave!

There was air inside the underwater cave, so the kids climbed out of the sub and went exploring.

"Hello!" Fred called. His voice echoed several times throughout the cave.

"Please don't do that, Fred," Shaggy said nervously. "Like, I'm afraid someone might answer!"

Scooby made a creepy discovery — skeletons dressed in armor!

"I think we've discovered a burial ground used by ancient Scottish warriors," Velma said.

"Well, if the skeletons are down here, that means there must be a secret passage back up to the surface," Daphne observed.

"Hey guys, check us out!" Shaggy and Scooby had put on some of the ancient armor. "We're a couple of brave warriors!"

"Reah, reah!" Scooby agreed.

But they weren't feeling very brave a moment later when the monster suddenly appeared!

"Jinkies!" Velma exclaimed.

"Everyone back into the submarine!" Fred yelled.

The angry monster chased after them as their sub once again dived deep underwater. Luckily, the little sub was fast and it maneuvered well. Soon they'd left the creature far behind.

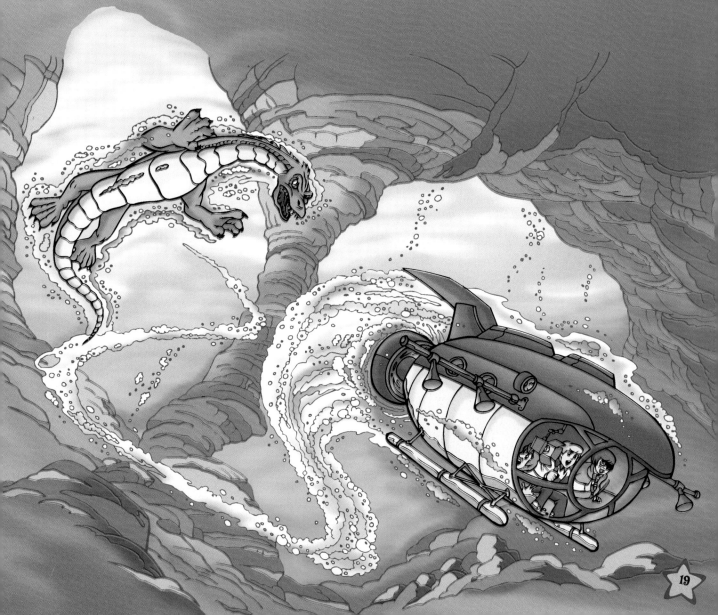

The Mystery, Inc. kids thought they'd seen the last of the monster for awhile. So that night they went into the forest to help Del find his van, which had been stolen. But they were in for a big surprise. Out of the woods came the creature, roaring and snapping at the Mystery Machine! ROAR!

"This is the moment I've been waiting for my whole life!" Del was overjoyed to finally meet the Loch Ness Monster.

Just then, the monster swerved, left the road, and came to a complete standstill.

"I think we need to take a closer look at this *monster*," Fred said.

The kids grabbed hold of the monster's skin and pulled. To everyone's amazement, the monster was made out of canvas. And it was attached to the top of Del's van! Del was sad for a moment because the beast wasn't real, but soon he cheered up since they'd found his missing van.

The gang realized they needed to see if the monster in the lake was a fake, too. Velma came up with a plan. Scooby and Shaggy rowed out onto the lake to attract the creature.

"Really, Scooby," Shaggy sighed. "Is there *anything* we won't do for some Scooby Snacks?"

"Ruh-uh!" Scooby shook his head as he gobbled down the treats.
Without warning, the Loch Ness Monster appeared right underneath them!
"Zoinks!" Shaggy cried. He and Scooby slid down the monster's back and
rushed all the way back to shore.

Getting back on dry land didn't help Shaggy and Scooby much. There was a second creature waiting for them there!

"Help! This place is infested with monsters!" Shaggy cried.

He and Scooby were so frightened, they forgot about the pit they'd dug earlier to catch the lake monster in.

"Guys, look out!" Velma called out. "That's where we set the trap!"
But it was too late. **FWOOM!** Scooby and Shaggy fell right into the deep
pit. The creature came to the edge of the trap and growled down at them.

Meanwhile, back at the lake, the first monster was on a rampage. It knocked Fred, Sir Ian, and Del into the water. And then the angry creature plunged Del's van into the water, too!

The creature moved close to Sir Ian and lifted its terrifying head out of the water.

"I don't believe it!" Sir Ian was astonished. "The monster *is* real!"

"Help! Throw me a line!" Sir Ian cried fearfully. "I can't swim!"

"We've got to do something!" Shannon exclaimed to Daphne.

The creature opened its mouth and looked like it was just about to gobble Sir Ian up. Daphne worked the controls of the ship's magnetic arm and picked the beast clean out of the water.

"Who ever heard of a magnet stopping a sea monster?" Shannon asked.

But there was no time to answer that question. Scooby and Shaggy were still in danger! Daphne swung the magnetic arm holding the creature and smashed it into the other monster, which was still standing over the trap. POW! The second creature was knocked into the pit!

"Scooby? Shaggy?" Velma ran up and looked down into the pit. "Are you guys okay?"

"Terrific, considering we're squashed under the Loch Ness Monster!" Shaggy hollered.

"Monster? I don't think so," Velma declared as Shaggy and Scooby quickly climbed out of the pit. "Take another look."

"Colin and Angus Haggard?" Shaggy asked.

"Roar?" said the brothers timidly. They had used their balloon to scare Scooby and Shaggy. They had also disguised Del's van to look like a sea creature. To them, it was all just a hilarious practical joke.

"So, if the monster in the pit is a fake, like, what about the other one?" Shaggy asked.

Daphne worked the controls of the magnetic arm. "Time for this monster to hit the beach!"

The creature fell down with a loud metallic clang. Part of its skin was peeled back, and they saw it was actually a robot. The gang cautiously approached as a big metal door in its side slowly opened.

"Professor Fiona Pembroke?" Fred exclaimed. Everyone was astonished.

"I just wanted to convince Sir Ian there really *is* a Loch Ness Monster," Professor Pembroke explained. "It was the only way he'd help me find the real one."

So the mystery was solved — and no one was in trouble. In fact, after examining Professor Pembroke's evidence, Sir Ian decided to help her hunt for the real Loch Ness Monster.

The Highland Games went off without a hitch, with sporting events, dancing, singing, and plenty of refreshments! The best part for Shaggy and Scooby was leading the parade.

"Like, I never thought being a drum major could be so . . . major!" Shaggy laughed.

"Rooby-rooby-roo!" Scooby-Doo cheered happily.